# SCHUMANN

## SCENES FROM CHILDHOOD

**OPUS 15**
**FOR THE PIANO**

EDITED BY WILLARD A. PALMER

## CONTENTS

Robert Schumann, Etching by L. Michalek.
By courtesy of the Library of Congress.

A CD recording of *Scenes from Childhood*, recorded by
Valery Lloyd-Watts, is available separately (#16794).

Second Edition

*Cover art:* Village Children
   *by John Singer Sargent (American, 1856–1925)*
   *Oil on canvas, 1890*
   *The Edwin Austin Abbey Memorial Collection*
   *Yale University Art Gallery, New Haven, Connecticut*

Title page of 1st edition 1839.
By courtesy of the Library of Congress.

# ORIGIN

Robert Schumann's Opus 15, *Scenes from Childhood* was begun in 1837, the year he became engaged to Clara Wieck.

In a letter to Clara dated February 11, 1838, Schumann wrote, "I have been waiting for your letter and consequently have composed books full of things—wonderful, crazy and solemn stuff; you will open your eyes when you come to play it. In fact, I sometimes feel simply bursting with music. But before I forget, let me tell you what else I have composed. Perhaps it was an echo of what you said to me once, that sometimes I seemed to you like a child; anyhow, I suddenly got an inspiration and knocked off about 30 quaint little things, from which I have selected twelve and called them *Kinderszenen*. They will amuse you, but of course you must forget you are a virtuoso. They all explain themselves, and what's more, they are as easy as possible."

Schumann actually selected *thirteen* of these pieces to make up the *Kinderszenen*, published in 1839 by Breitkopf & Härtel. The selections are not programme music in the strictest sense. The poetic titles were found, Schumann himself stated, after the work was written. When someone gave an explanation of one of the pieces, Schumann said, "I suppose he thinks I visualize a crying child and then try to find the right notes. Just the opposite is the case."

In spite of Schumann's remarks concerning the simplicity of the *Scenes from Childhood*, some of the pieces make considerable technical demands upon the performer, particularly when played at tempos indicated by the composer. Many virtuoso pianists have performed the entire opus as a concert offering. When the work is performed as a whole, each individual selection leads directly into the next with a unity rarely found in a collection of separate pieces.

# SOURCES FOR THIS EDITION

The autographs are not the important sources for *Scenes from Childhood*. The few that remain are in the form of preliminary sketches. They are interesting, but they do not present the composer's final intentions. One early sketch shows that the melody of the most popular work of the set, *Träumerei*, was first conceived as follows:

The sources used in the preparation of this edition are:

1. All the autographs known to exist; by courtesy of the Library of Congress, Washington, D.C., and the Robert Schumann Museum, Zwickau, Germany.

2. A copy of the first printing of the first edition, courtesy of the Library of Congress.
3. A copy of the second printing of the first edition, courtesy of the Library of Congress.
4. The Clara Schumann edition, published by Breitkopf & Härtel.

The first printing of the first edition (Breitkopf & Härtel, 1839) must have been disappointing to Schumann. Some of the slurs did not clearly indicate which notes were encompassed, some accent marks were poorly engraved, some staccato marks were missing. For the second printing the plates were reworked. In this printing, the slurs and accents are clear and the missing staccato marks added. Thus, the second printing of the first edition is the most important source available.

## PHRASING, DYNAMICS AND PEDALING

Few editorial suggestions are needed in the *Scenes from Childhood*. Schumann was reasonably careful in marking the phrasing and dynamics. Pedal indications, however, are of a very general nature. At the beginning of each selection he wrote the symbol 𝄡 below the first measure, but showed no release following it. This is the equivalent of *con pedale* and only indicates he wanted the pedal to be used, but at the discretion of the performer. Only in a few measures did he give specific pedal indications. These appear in the present edition in dark print.

## ORNAMENTATION

Only a few ornaments, mostly appoggiaturas and turns, are used in *Scenes from Childhood*. These are played in the conventional manner. There are no trills.

## TEMPO

Some of the tempos in *Scenes from Childhood* are controversial. While Schumann provided metronome markings for each piece, several of these indications are difficult to accept. We have never heard an artist play *Träumerei* at M.M. ♩ = 100. It is generally played at about half that tempo. Even Clara Schumann, who often played too fast to please Robert, changed this indication to ♩ = 80. *Pleading Child* is certainly unconvincing at Schumann's indicated M.M. ♪ = 138. Clara changed this to ♪ = 88. On the other hand, some of Clara's tempos are faster than Robert's.

It is certain that these selections find much more practical use as teaching pieces when slower tempos are used. The tempo indications in light print at the beginning of each selection are intended to provide a practical solution for most teaching situations.

The following tempo table is compiled from the two important editions and from recorded performances of various artists. In some cases, the tempos taken from recordings are approximate, because of the rubato used by the artists.

| | M.M. | EDITIONS | | RECORDINGS | | | | |
| --- | --- | --- | --- | --- | --- | --- | --- | --- |
| | | 1st Edition | Clara Schumann | Clara Haskil | Vladimir Horowitz | Benno Moiseiwitsch | Guiomar Novaes | Alexis Weissenberg |
| 1. About Strange Lands and People | ♩ | 108 | 108 | 69 | 72 | 52 | 80 | 48 |
| 2. Curious Story | ♩ | 112 | 132 | 138 | 132 | 132 | 126 | 132 |
| 3. Catch Me! | ♩ | 138 | 120 | 140 | 132 | 138 | 126 | 144 |
| 4. Pleading Child | ♪ | 138 | 88 | 116 | 96 | 104 | 84 | 116 |
| 5. Perfect Happiness | ♪ | 132 | 144 | 192 | 152 | 184 | 152 | 216 |
| 6. Important Event | ♩ | 138 | 120 | 144 | 144 | 116 | 116 | 80 |
| 7. Reverie (Träumerei) | ♩ | 100 | 80 | 56 | 52 | 54 | 58 | 48 |
| 8. By the Fireside | ♩ | 138 | 108 | 138 | 100 | 120 | 126 | 120 |
| 9. Knight of the Rocking-Horse | ♩. | 80 | 76 | 96 | 84 | 80 | 72 | 104 |
| 10. Almost Too Serious | ♩ | 69 | 52 | 60 | 53 | 48 | 42 | 69 |
| 11. Frightening | ♩ | 96 | 108 | 84 | 84 | 80 | 76 | 56 |
| 12. Child Falling Asleep | ♪ | 92 | 80 | 92 | 92 | 84 | 76 | 63 |
| 13. The Poet Speaks | ♩ | 112 | 92 | 69 | 92 | 72 | 72 | 46 |

*A list of recordings from which these metronome markings were derived will be found on page 32.*

# 1. About Strange Lands and People

Von fremden Ländern und Menschen

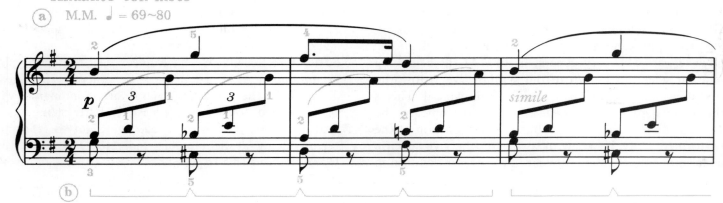

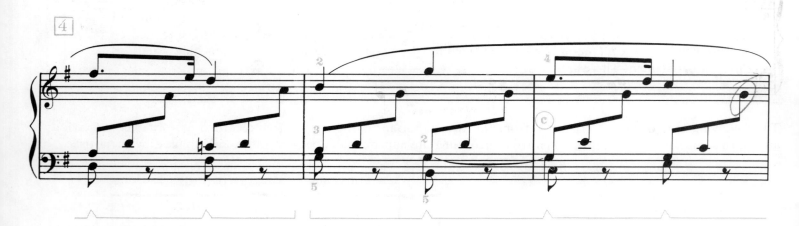

 The first edition and the Clara Schumann edition have M.M. ♩ = 108. See the table on page 3.

 The first edition indicates only 𝕻𝖊𝖉. at the beginning, meaning *con pedale*.

 The quarter note downstem on the G is missing here in the first edition; probably an oversight, since it is present in measure 20.

# 2. Curious Story

Kuriose Geschichte

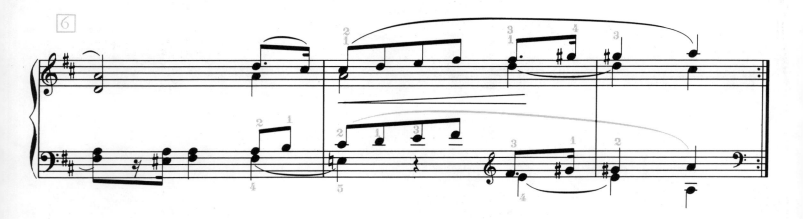

(a) The first edition has M.M. ♩ = 112. The Clara Schumann edition has ♩ = 132.

(b) The Clara Schumann edition has *mf–piú* **p**.

(c) 🎵, meaning *con pedale*, is from the first edition. The Clara Schumann edition contains no pedal indications. The pedaling here is left to the individual.

(d) The appoggiatura is played *on the beat*, as quickly as possible.

(e) *Molto legato* is from the Clara Schumann edition.

# 3. Catch Me!

Hasche-Mann

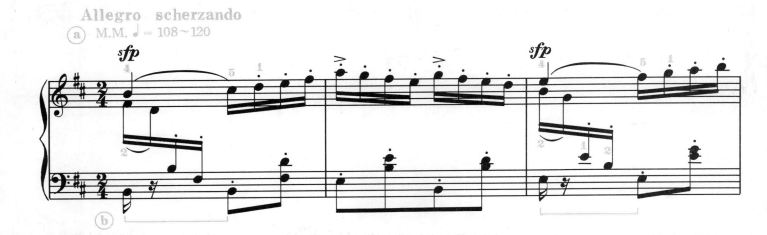

(a) The first edition has M.M. ♩ = 138. The Clara Schumann edition has ♩ = 120.

(b) The first edition indicates only 🎵 at the beginning, meaning *con pedale*. The pedal indications in light print are from the Clara Schumann edition.

9

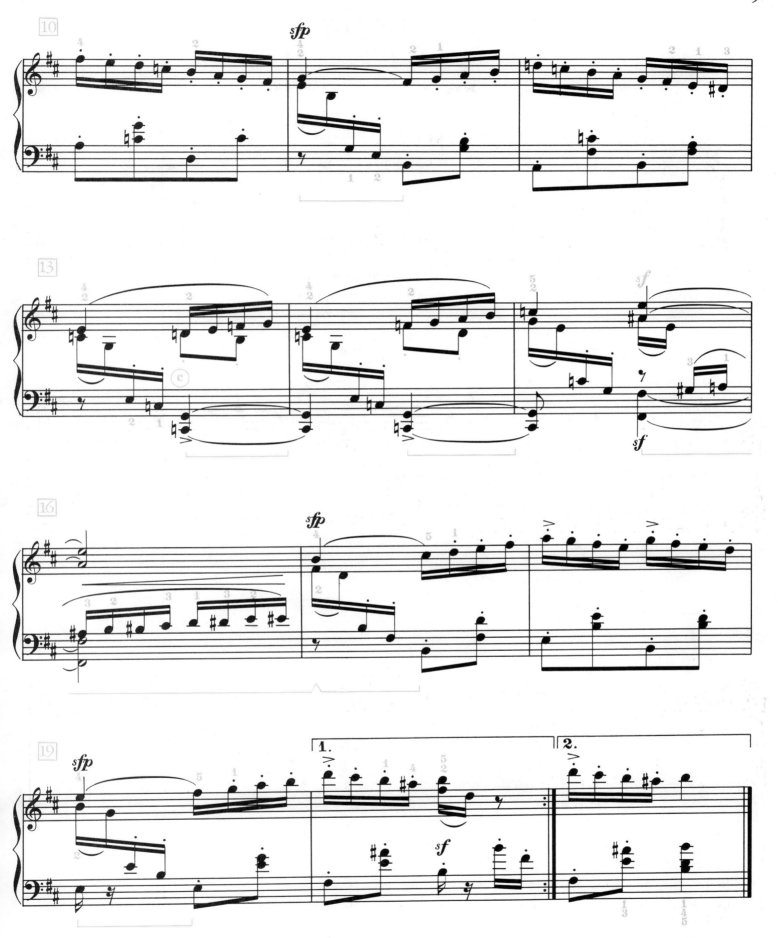

# 4. Pleading Child

### Bittendes Kind

(a) The first edition has M.M. ♪ = 138. The Clara Schumann edition has ♪ = 88.

(b) The first edition has 𝓟𝓮𝓭 at the beginning, meaning *con pedale*. The pedal indications in light print are by the editor. The Clara Schumann edition has a pedal indication only on the first count of measures 1, 3, 5, 7, 13 & 15, and a pedal indication from the last half of measure 16 to the end of the piece.

(c) The *una corda* and *tre corda* indications are from the Clara Schumann edition.

# 5. Perfect Happiness

Glückes genug

ⓐ The first edition has M.M. ♪ = 132. The Clara Schumann edition has ♩ = 72 (♪ = 144).

ⓑ The first edition has 🎵 at the beginning and below the first note of measure 9 and measure 17, but no releases are indicated. The pedal indications in light print are from the Clara Schumann edition.

# 6. Important Event

## Wichtige Begebenheit

ⓐ The first edition has M.M. ♩ = 138. The Clara Schumann edition has ♩ = 120.

ⓑ The first edition has the usual *con pedale* indication. The Clara Schumann edition has no pedal indications.

# 7. Reverie

Träumerei

The first edition has M.M. ♩ = 100. The Clara Schumann edition has ♩ = 80.

The first edition has 𝒫𝑒𝑑., meaning *con pedale*. The pedal indications in light print are from the Clara Schumann edition.

© The first edition has 🎹 at each of these places, but no release is shown.

18

# 8. By the Fireside

Am Kamin

ⓐ The first edition has M.M. ♩ = 138. The Clara Schumann edition has ♩ =108.

ⓑ The first edition has only the usual indication signifying *con pedale*. The pedal indications in light print are from the Clara Schumann edition.

# 9. Knight of the Rocking-Horse

### Ritter vom Steckenpferd

The title may be related to an incident that happened in 1836. Herr Ritter von Ritterstein made a visit to hear Clara play but did not want to hear any of Schumann's music because he "expected the composer to play it so much better." After hearing her play he begged her to play something by Schumann because the composer had so kindly referred him to Clara.

(a)  The first edition has M.M. ♩· = 80. The Clara Schumann edition has ♩· = 76.

(b)  The first edition has 𝄢, meaning *con pedale*. The pedal indications in light print are by the editor.

(c)  The *f* is from the autograph, which also shows a crescendo beginning at the 10th measure and continuing to *ff* in the 14th measure.

# 10. Almost Too Serious

Fast zu ernst

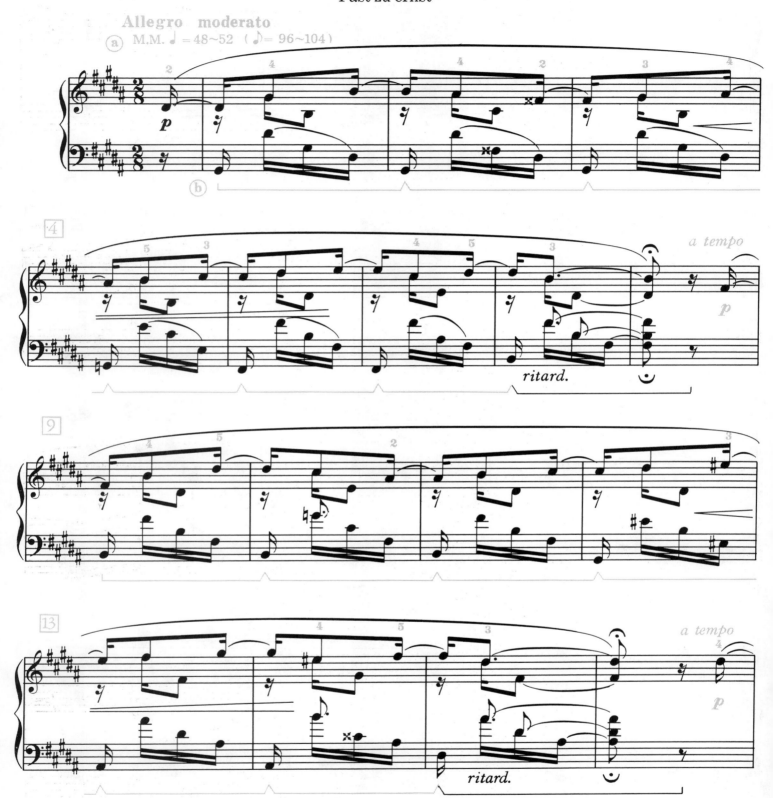

(a) The first edition has M.M. ♩ = 69. The Clara Schumann edition has ♪ =104 (♩ = 52).

(b) The first edition has 𝄢, indicating *con pedale*. The pedal indications in light print are from the Clara Schumann edition.

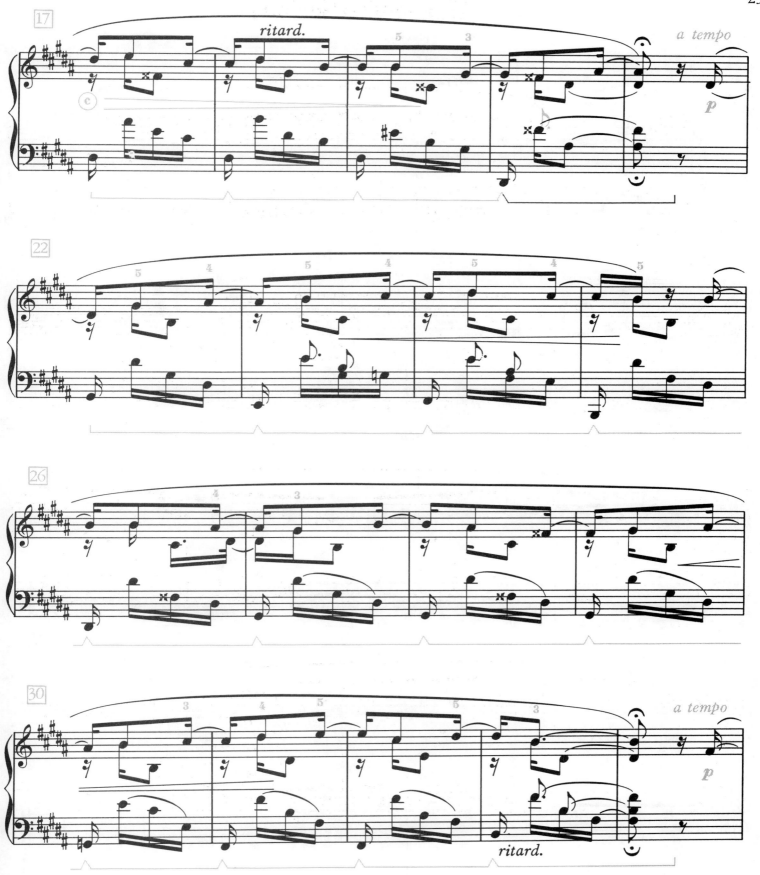

Ⓒ The diminuendo is from the Clara Schumann edition.

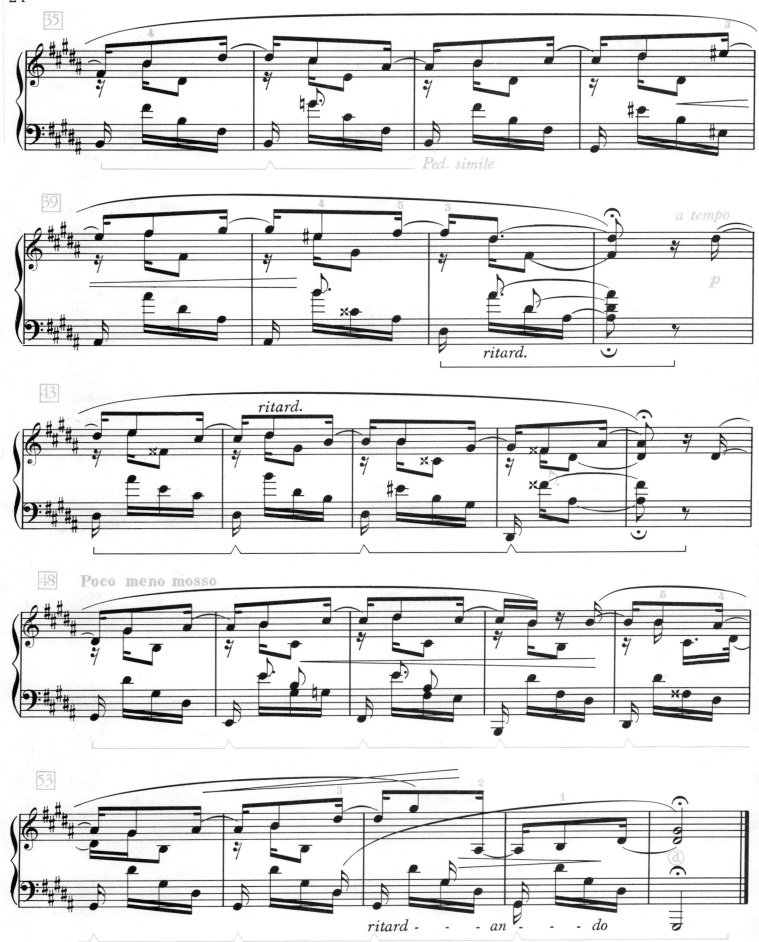

(d) The half notes appear in the original edition. Schumann may have used them to indicate a very long fermata.

# 11. Frightening

Fürchtenmachen

(a) The first edition has M.M. ♩ = 96. The Clara Schumann edition has ♩ = 108.

(b) The first edition has 𝄐, meaning *con pedale*. The pedal indications in light print are from the Clara Schumann edition.

(c) The first edition has *Schneller* here and in measure 37. No metronome indication is given. The Clara Schumann edition has M.M. ♩ = 132.

(d) The Clara Schumann edition continues the slur to the last L.H. note of the measure, here and in measure 40.

(e) *Tempo primo* here and in measure 41 is from the Clara Schumann edition.

(f) *Non legato* is from the Clara Schumann edition.

# 12. Child Falling Asleep

### Kind im Einschlummern

(a) The first edition has M.M. ♪ = 92. The Clara Schumann edition has ♪ = 80.

(b) The first edition has 𝆓, meaning *con pedale*, here and at the beginning of the 9th measure. The pedal indications in light print are from the Clara Schumann edition.

# 13. The Poet Speaks

Der Dichter spricht

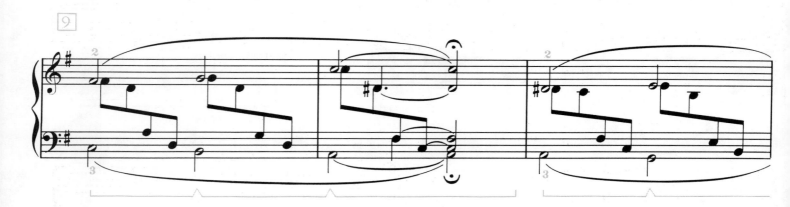

(a) The first edition has M.M. ♩ = 112. The Clara Schumann edition has ♩ = 92.

(b) The first edition has 🎵, meaning *con pedale*. The pedal indications in light print are by the editor.

(c) The Clara Schumann edition has the footnote "this turn is played very calmly."

(d) Original notation:    Clara Schumann edition:

The omission of the A is undoubtedly an error.

## RECOMMENDED RECORDINGS

| | | |
|---|---|---|
| HASKIL, CLARA | Epic | Record No. LC 3358 |
| HOROWITZ, VLADIMIR | Columbia | Record No. MS 6411 |
| MOISEIWITSCH, BENNO | Decca | Record No. DL 711048 |
| NOVAES, GUIOMAR | Turnabout Vox | Record No. TV 341645 |
| WEISSENBERG, ALEXIS | Angel | Record No. S 36616 |

---

## RECOMMENDED READING

Chissell, Joan.
SCHUMANN, Collier Books, New York, 1962.

A well-written biography seeking the intrinsic connections between the composer's music and his personal life.

Schauffler, Robert Haven.
FLORESTAN: THE LIFE AND WORK OF ROBERT SCHUMANN, Dover Publications, Inc., New York, 1963.

Probably the best study of Schumann in the English language.

Schumann, Robert.
ON MUSIC AND MUSICIANS, translated by Paul Rosenfeld, McGraw-Hill Book Co., New York, 1946, paperback edition 1964.

Schumann was one of the great writers on music. The study of his views on the music of other musicians of his day gives valuable insight for the performance of his own works. Of particular interest to students are his *Aphorisms*, which he calls "House Rules and Maxims for Young Musicians."

---

## ACKNOWLEDGMENTS

I would like to express my thanks to Irving Chasnov and Morton Manus of Alfred Music Company for the meticulous care with which they helped to prepare this edition. I also wish to thank Judith Simon Linder for her valuable assistance in the research necessary for the realization of this edition and for her help in preparing the manuscript.